Complete Me

A 1Night Stand Story

By
Catherine Peace

This book is a work of fiction. Names, characters, places, and incidents are the products of the author's imagination or used fictitiously. Any resemblance to actual events, locales or persons, living or dead, is entirely coincidental.

Published by
Decadent Publishing Company, LLC

Look for us online at:
www.decadentpublishing.com

Dedication

Thank you to my BFF Connie Smith, for writing and perfecting the songs in this book. Without you, Ty wouldn't have a song to sing.

Chapter One

"You did *what?* "

Of all things to suggest. Of all the backhanded, dirty things to do. If Penelope Birchfield hadn't been one of the best PR people in the business, Claire would've strangled the woman through the phone. This topped every ploy Penny had used to get books on shelves and into readers' hands. Every single, solitary one.

"It'll be good for you," the PR maven said. "I've been working with you for five years now, and in each interview, you've danced around the *significant other* question. I got tired of it. It's not helping your image."

Ah, yes. The Holy Image could not be tarnished. Not like Claire didn't have a perfectly good reason for staying single.

"You're in the public eye too much not to have something steady. I mean, really, how many best-selling romance authors do you know who don't even date?"

With enough time, Claire could find a suitable response. Right then, Penelope had her too flustered to think straight. "I'm busy all the time, thanks to a certain somebody."

"Yeah, you should really fire that bitch."

"I should. Definitely." It wasn't entirely Claire's fault her Prohibition-era series, set in the Windy City and inspired by the still-popular 1970s band Chicago, had done so well. She stared at the text of *All Roads Lead to You*, her latest, and sighed. "In the meantime, I have edits to finish."

"Noooo, you have a date to get ready for. I sent his profile to your private e-mail. You should probably look it over."

While she still had Penny on the phone, Claire accessed her seldom-used account. "If this guy is anything less than perfect...."

"I think you'll be pleasantly surprised."

She pulled up the e-mail and opened the attachment, labeled, *1Night Stand—Claire Greene*. After a few moments, her date's profile dominated her laptop screen. *Dear God, there's every romance writer's dream.* Ty Krause's photo alone had her salivating thanks to a sexy rocker look, dark hair, intense stare, and the most beautiful eyes she'd ever seen, more like mahogany than true brown. "He has a lip ring."

"Yes, he does."

"You might have mentioned that." Only Penny knew about Claire's peculiar fetish. The silver ring accented his lower lip, which she'd already imagined nibbling on. "I still don't think this is a good idea."

"No, it's not a good idea. It's a fantastic idea."

"How'd you hear about this company anyway?" In the last few years, she'd been goaded into trying every dating service known to man, but somehow,

1Night Stand had escaped everyone's attention.

"Teri recommended it."

Claire almost imagined the nonchalant shrug that must have followed Penny's statement.

"Teri Carr?"

"The very same."

The one who'd rocketed up both *USA Today and The New York Times*' best-seller lists within the last couple of months?

"Are you still there?"

"Y-yeah. Sorry. Having a writer moment."

The other woman grunted. "Right now you need to have a woman moment. Read Ty's profile and figure out what you're wearing, princess."

Princess. Like she caused so much trouble. "Yes, wicked stepmother."

"Aww, aren't I the fairy godmother?"

"We'll see."

***

Ty's profile contained everything she needed to know. A thirty-two-year-old Charleston native, a musician—*score*—with sexual interests similar to hers, none of which were horribly kinky. The more she read, the more she liked, but she couldn't stop wondering why his name sounded so familiar. Google told her after a few keystrokes—he'd been the bassist and main songwriter of an early-2000s hard- rock band, Dejected, which had one hit, penned by said bassist, and received serious airtime on pop stations. She vaguely recalled the tune, though she couldn't remember the lyrics. Currently, he wrote songs for some teenybopper band from England that probably used them to get laid.

Talk about a fall from grace. She understood sacrifice, though. *You have to go where the money is.*

Clicking on the e-mail again, she jotted the details on her desktop calendar. *It's one night.* What harm could it really do? Besides, it'd be something fun to talk about in interviews.

Yeah. This could be good. Maybe a little actual romance in her life would translate to her characters'. For some reason, Trace and Ella still wouldn't cooperate even after multiple rounds of edits and her third extended deadline loomed on the horizon. If she begged her publisher to postpone the release again, she could very well lose her contract. Claire had to make the scene sing. It set up the climax of the story.

Closing the document, she decided to give in to the girly need to raid her closet for a suitable outfit. How often did a romance author get to have dinner with a sexy songwriter? Then she thought about the photo. She had his, so he'd have to have hers, right? *Time for a phone call.*

Before Penelope could say hello, Claire said, "Which photo did you send?"

"What?"

"With the profile. Which photo did you send?

"I didn't use any of your author shots, if that's what you're worried about. Your sister sent me one she liked."

"Oh, God. You let Sheila decide? You really are the wicked stepmother."

"It's a nice picture. Very flattering."

"E-vil."

Penny sighed. "Have you found an outfit yet?"

Claire rolled her eyes. "I'm. Looking."

"Look harder, and don't call me until you have something to report."

Wicked, evil, insufferable stepmother, indeed.

Chapter Two

Ty fingered the bass and tried to push the newest bullshit melody he'd written for Sleeping Angels out of his mind. Bunch of twerps. What the hell business did fifteen-year-olds have making music? Shouldn't they be in school? Or at least back in England and far away from him?

Didn't help that their dumb-as-fuck manager did stupid shit, like buy them all alcohol the night before their last performance. Theo—nicknamed *Shy One* for some ungodly reason—had been slightly drunk when they'd performed and botched every word. Not like Ty put a ton of big words into their songs, but still. A musical massacre like that would hurt anybody. At least Sleeping Angels were on tour and out of his hair for a while so he could remember what real music sounded like.

The only consolation: they paid well. More than well. And they got played like nobody's business on the radio. Every other song the previous summer had been "Seize the Summer" and the royalties had paid for his cozy Kiawah Island beach house, which he used as a hideaway-slash-studio. Whoever conceptualized private beaches needed to come over for drinks.

Instead, he jammed on a nice solo session, a combination of a few of his band's old songs and something he hadn't gotten out of his head quite yet. It'd started as a few chords, which he'd banged out on the keyboard, but refused to go any further than that. What he'd played so far that day hadn't given him any breakthroughs. Creative limbo hell had closed its gates and locked him in. And when that happened, his mind always turned to Jocelyn.

It'd been almost ten years since she'd left, but no matter what he did, he couldn't get her out of his mind. Joss had been his muse, his true love, his everything, and when she walked away, he'd crumbled like the pathetic POS he was. He couldn't make it without her. Dejected fell apart, and he took to writing songs for whiny teenage boys to make ends meet.

And hadn't had a girlfriend since.

He'd barely managed two friends-with-benefits situations over the years. They'd been good—Brielle had been great—but they'd done nothing to fill the hole left by his muse. Sometimes, he heard part of "Beautiful Blaze" on the radio and turned the sound off altogether. He'd written the music for Joss, written the lyrics so she'd know exactly how much he loved her, and she'd walked out anyway. For all his bravado, his heart could not say "Fuck that bitch" like his mouth had been able to.

He'd tried a few dating sites, too, and come up empty. His last resort had been Madame Eve's 1Night Stand, and while another one-night stand was the last thing he needed, it'd break the monotony. Graeme,

Dejected's guitarist and Ty's one friend, had suggested the service, said it'd worked wonders for a friend or cousin, or somebody. Couldn't hurt, right?

With that thought, he begrudgingly stepped back inside. The cool air from the A/C chilled him for a moment, but he shook it off. The background of his computer showed the last time he'd been truly happy—Dejected's final concert. He and Graeme had been involved in an epic guitar duet that had lasted almost ten minutes and energized the crowd to the point its roar drowned out the monitors, and he'd never felt more alive. Like living electricity.

Then Joss left him for Anderson, the drummer, and Dejected never played again.

Pushing the memory aside, Ty opened his in-box. Buried in the avalanche of unread messages, he found one from Madame Eve.

He opened the e-mail before he bitched out of it. The text contained the necessary information, which he'd note later. Right then, he wanted to see the profile.

When it loaded, his date's smile, so carefree and beautiful, caught his attention. She looked like she'd been in the middle of laughing, and at that moment he decided it'd be his mission to hear that laugh, see that kind of joy light up her face.

Then he noticed her eyes, some shade of aquamarine he'd never seen on another person. They were clear, like the waters of the Mediterranean, full of mischief and secrets. He grazed his fingertips over the photo, wondering if her porcelain skin would be as smooth as it looked, if the Cupid's-bow mouth would taste as sweet as he imagined.

His cell phone rang. Trance broken, he glanced

at the screen and a jolt rocketed through his body. Why now? He debated letting it go to voice-mail, but when Jocelyn wanted something, she could be relentless.

"Hey, Joss."

Without humor, she chuckled. "Ty. I heard you're all alone."

Ah, their code. If either of them said they were alone, the other would come to the rescue. Most of the time, he did the rescuing. He rolled his eyes. "What do you want?"

"Just wanted to see how you were."

Translation: she wanted to make sure he still missed her. "Actually, I'm kind of busy right now." While he looked over the date details, he tuned her out. They'd played this stupid game for so long, it'd become an almost ritualistic part of his life, and he'd let it. He shouldered his half of the blame, but a small part of him still desperately needed his ex in his life, in whatever capacity he could have, even if all he got was this. Stupid as it sounded, he'd never given up hope someday they could try again. Maybe, after tonight, he would.

"Doing what?"

To tell her, or not to tell her.... "I scored a gig at a small bar. Acoustic set."

"Aww, well, good for you."

"Thanks. So I have to go get ready. Sound check's in an hour."

He ended the call before she had a chance to toss in how much Anderson's new band loved their current European tour.

Life had more to offer than this; it had to. So what if he didn't play large venues anymore? His life brought him satisfaction. Mostly.

Running a hand through his hair, he pushed Joss from his mind. After all, he had a beautiful woman to get ready for.

And, hopefully, she wouldn't be batshit crazy.

Chapter Three

Claire had heard of "musician time," but as she checked her watch to discover she was thirty minutes late, she wondered if Ty knew anything about "author time." Her hero, Trace, had *finally* gotten past his hang-ups and asked Ella to dance in the new scene she'd plotted. The deadline for their story loomed over her head like a storm cloud ready to unleash the heavens.

Smoothing her dress, she approached the maître d'. "Jada—er, Claire Greene." So *weird* giving her real name for something anymore.

With a polite smile, the older gentleman led her past tables filled with happy couples, seated next to each other with barely any space between them, unaware of anyone else in the room. Some were deep in conversation, and others appeared to be enjoying their golden years with glasses of wine and laughter, almost as oblivious as the younger couples. She headed toward the partitioned area of the restaurant, marked *private*.

She shivered, and not from the cool air circulating through the room. The anticipation, the excitement, the miniscule amount of dread, all caused her to tremble. But nothing had prepared her for the man sitting at the only table there, situated in front of the enormous bay window. When he spotted them, he stood and smiled, looking her up and down with a beautiful mahogany stare. The maître d' dipped his head and left.

"Ty," she said. One word took every bit of her concentration. He'd dressed in a way she defined as *rock-star chic*. White shirt, black tie, black blazer with sleeves that stopped at his muscular forearms, tight-fitting dress trousers, and a black-and-white checkered fedora with a black band. On any other person, it probably would have looked ridiculous, but on him? Just right.

"Claire. A pleasure to meet you." He planted a small kiss on her knuckles. Then he walked around her and pulled a chair out. "You look beautiful."

Dear, sweet baby Jesus. Forming coherent sentences would be the least of her challenges that night. "Thank you. You look…." As a thousand adjectives tumbled through her overstimulated brain, he simply smiled. She wondered if the look on her face said what her mouth couldn't.

Then he removed the hat and swept a hand through shoulder-length hair she wanted to play with. "I started to think you wouldn't show."

She laughed, too loudly, considering her nerves. "I'm sorry. I got swept up in work."

"It happens."

The next couple of hours passed almost in a daydream. They discussed their similar interests—a love of action flicks and Bruce Willis, music, reading, the outdoors—and shared a few somewhat embarrassing stories. She told him about her books, and he talked a little about his band, but without the enthusiasm she'd expected. *Hiding something?*

"How about heading upstairs?" he asked after dessert. "The room is...pretty spectacular."

And it was.

Typical of Charleston, the suite had been decorated in subtle creams, yellows, and light and navy blues to provide a nautical feel. Straight ahead, a small seating area with a sand-colored couch, dark end tables, and a large flat-screen TV in a matching cabinet took up a quarter of the actual space. And, of course, situated as a focal point in the room, a fireplace. Not like it'd be cool enough to warrant a fire, but somehow the room would have been incomplete without it.

To her right, in its own nook, sat the bed, a large four-poster dressed in luxurious mother-of-pearl silk. A cornflower-blue chenille throw with the Castillo logo covered the foot. She spared a quick glance at her date. He watched her, unabashedly, and her face heated. So what if she thought about having sex with him? That was part of why she'd agreed to their date. Well, why Penny had agreed to it on her behalf, anyway.

Then she noticed the balcony, complete with wrought iron railing. As a child, she'd been fascinated with that particular ornate detail work, a part of the city's charm. She loved the designs, the grace and strength of the metal, and had hoped to have a house full of it someday. Of course, then she'd grown up, and her current residence in St. Matthews had none of the Lowcountry's decorative charm. Instead, her place was magazine chic, as though no one lived there at all. In some ways, no one really did.

Claire stepped onto the balcony. Traffic and horse-drawn carriages carrying tourists filled the street below. Even downtown, the salt-and-brine ocean scent overpowered the other scents of car exhaust and horses. A light breeze drifted from the water, tousling her hair. She lived not an hour away yet she'd forgotten how much she loved Charleston—its sights, sounds, smells, and history. And life. When had she forgotten how to live?

A solid form came up behind her. Ty rested his hands on the railing, pinning her against it. She noted his toned forearms and the black ink disappearing beneath his right shirtsleeve. Whatever Madame Eve had been thinking, picking him...Claire owed the woman a thank-you letter. *Thank you for getting me to live again.*

His cologne tickled her nose, a spicy, masculine scent with hints of cedar. Unwilling to have any space between them, she leaned back until the hard muscles of his chest and stomach molded to her, and an unmistakable, hardening erection pressed into her ass. He brushed her hair from her neck and brushed his lips against the sensitive skin, his scruff adding a hint of pain to the pleasure.

And then his cell rang.

Ty took a deep breath and removed the evil contraption from his pocket. It blared Jet's "Cold, Hard Bitch."

"Fuck. I'm sorry. I need to take this."

"Sure, no problem."

While he directed his attention to the phone call, she focused on the sounds around her to slow her erratic heartbeat: the clomping of hooves on the cobblestone streets, the chatter from passersby, seagull cries. She studied the flowers and trees in the park across the street, which boasted beautiful weeping willows, their drooping foliage nearly shielding an old fountain.

But Ty's raised voice pulled her away from the sights around her. *What on earth?* Her blood started to boil. At least she'd put her cell on silent, mostly so Penny wouldn't interrupt five hundred times, and Claire expected the same courtesy from him. Slowly, the blinders dropped from her eyes. Maybe Madame Eve's thank-you letter would have to wait.

Another few minutes passed, with Ty's tone growing more heated with each passing second. *Enough.* She'd had an idea for the scene in *All Roads Lead to You* that had been giving her fits. Trace and Ella were officially calling her name, and working on their story held more appeal than listening to an argument.

While his back was turned, she grabbed her purse and headed toward the door. As her hand landed on the doorknob and she swore never to listen to Penelope again, he cursed behind her. A soft thump indicated he'd probably tossed the cell phone on a nearby cushion.

"I am so sorry, Claire."

"Whatever," she said, inwardly cringing at sounding like a petulant teenager. "I have work to do." She turned toward him. "And it sounds like you have business to attend to."

He scraped a palm over his face, still hot as hell even in distress. "I'm sorry. It was.... Joss. My ex."

Her heart almost stopped. A warning bell sounded in her mind, reminding her of the night she'd walked in on her then-boyfriend Neil—the only man she'd ever truly loved and wanted to be with forever—and *his* ex in a highly compromising position. As a result, the ultimate deal breaker for her had become a man maintaining contact with an ex-girlfriend. "As I said. Goodnight, Ty."

"Wait." The simple word froze her. Or maybe not the word, but the force of emotion behind it. The imploring tone.

Like an idiot, she set her purse on the floor. "Fine. But I think you owe me an explanation, and it better be a damn good one."

Damn it, Joss. Ty gestured toward the dinette near the balcony. Claire sat and crossed her long legs, pretty face in a scowl, her aquamarine eyes full of fire. Unable to think, he stayed rooted in place, feeling like shit.

"Joss is a long story." *Wow. Lame.*

"We've got plenty of time. Sit. Talk."

No, not plenty of time. One night. Obeying the order, he said, "Please, can we not discuss it?" He took her hand, rubbed small circles on the soft skin with the pad of his thumb. "I'd really like to get to know you."

She smiled without any real warmth. "The first thing you need to know is that I don't deal with bullshit." Gently, she pulled away from him then crossed her arms on the tabletop. "You should have been honest with me downstairs and told me you had a girlfriend."

"She's not my girlfriend. And I really didn't think she'd call." He'd said that plenty of times to plenty of would-be dates. "It won't happen again." *Not tonight.*

I hope.

"If that's true, turn off your phone."

Missing one of Jocelyn's calls almost caused his heart to stop. He hadn't missed a single one in ten years. Pathetic didn't even begin to describe him. But before he changed his mind, he retrieved the phone from the couch where he'd thrown it and did as she'd asked. "Done." *There.* When he looked up, a genuine smile graced Claire's face. Much better.

"Now, tell me the story. The real version."

Phew. Tall order. "How about I make a deal with you?"

"Okay...."

"I'm not feeling this room right now. How about we find a place to unwind?" Sounded much better than: *I need lots of alcohol to even begin talking about shit with Jocelyn Richards.*

Claire looked him over once before nodding. "Sure. I think I know the right place."

Chapter Four

The "right place" turned out to be a dive bar a few blocks from the hotel, much like the hundreds his band had played in before getting signed. Ty swallowed and held the door open for Claire, wondering what sort of evil woman would bring him to a place where someone might recognize him. He'd spent the years between 1997 and 2003 as a local Charleston celebrity, enjoying free drinks and plenty of adoration from the hard-rocking ladies in town.

Back then, he'd wanted to be well-known. Tonight, he wanted to make it through without someone asking him to sing "Beautiful Blaze." In the past, a few, usually drunk, patrons had begged him to sing it, and he'd acquiesced with the hope he'd never have to sing it again. But he wouldn't this time, not with the beautiful author on his arm. Joss needed to stay in distant memory, though the low-cost gear on the stage didn't give him much hope. Especially since the bass drum head read *Infamous Goat*. They were all reminders of the old days, back when he and Jocelyn had been happy, playing gigs in dimly lit bars with bands with funny names before Dejected took off and everything fell apart.

As a classic country drinking song blared from the jukebox, they found a table and he counted his blessings that none of the patrons had even looked their way. He settled Claire and got her drink order, then approached the bar, heart hammering like a double-bass drum in his throat. Had he been in this particular place before? In his early years of heavy drinking, every bar looked the same, and while he'd seriously cut back on the booze, most bartenders had memories like elephants. The one behind the counter might recognize him.

He tapped on the bar to get the chick's attention. Once upon a time, he would have hit on her, but even if he weren't on a date, this woman reminded him too much of Jocelyn. Her jet-black hair matched the smudged black eyeliner and emerald eye shadow accented deep-set hazel eyes. With her sloped nose and high cheekbones, she could have been his ex's twin.

She snapped her gaze from the customer she'd been talking to and focused—really focused in that scrutinizing way he hated—on him. Raising a pierced eyebrow, she propped her arms on the bar and tipped forward, giving him an eyeful of her corset-enhanced cleavage. "What can I get you?"

"Jack and Coke, and a Bud."

"Heavy drinker, huh?" She grinned.

He waited until she'd poured Claire's drink before saying, "One's for me. One's for my date." With as many bartenders as he'd flirted with to get free drinks, he couldn't blame her for trying to get a good tip, which she would anyway. After thanking her, he returned to the table, where his gorgeous date waited with a smile and twinkling eyes.

"Thank you. Now, I think it's story time."

"Is this a writer thing? Being persistent?" he asked, half-joking.

"No, this is a woman thing, which is worse. So, spill." Puckering her lips around the itty-bitty straw, she took a long drink, and for a moment his brain stopped working. When she set the glass back on the table and turned big, beautiful, shining eyes back to his, he remembered what he should be talking about—the long story that had spanned the last ten years.

He downed half the beer before speaking again. "Why the hell do you care so much?"

"Because this woman has disrupted our date once already. I deserve to know why you let her."

Damn. Verbal slap. No one ever asked "why" before. Joss had been in his life so long, he saw her as a natural phenomenon. Like thunderstorms, hurricanes, or blizzards, her calls happened, and he had to stay prepared. He'd never considered an alternative.

"Joss is like a wildfire," he said, staring into the bottle. If he looked into Claire's eyes right then, he'd fumble. "She takes hold, consumes, and you never wanted anything else. She started coming to shows with the girl who worked our merch table. We hit it off, and I fell in love.

"She started booking us bigger gigs, better ones. Stuff I couldn't believe. Opening for national acts, playing at Bonnaroo, awesome shit that we never imagined. When we got signed, she came on tour with us." He shrugged and took another swig. "I loved her more than I loved the band. I wrote our one big song for her. Then I learned the hard way that a fire like that can't be contained. She moved on. The band broke up. But, for some reason, I can't let her go. We were together for years and she's a part of my life. A toxic part, maybe...." Finally, he met Claire's intense gaze. "She still lives in nearby Hanahan, so we're only an hour apart. Even saying all of this sounds stupid, but there you have it."

"You still love her?"

He shook his head. "No. It's fucking pathetic, I know. I just—"

She placed a hand on his forearm. "I get it. I do. Some people are difficult to leave behind."

"Yeah." He had to be the dumbest asshole on Earth. Thank God the band on stage started up right then, all eyes on the next generation, saving him from admitting more stupidity. Hopefully the *Joss* conversation wouldn't have to happen again. He'd bought some time by taking her last call, but how much?

He focused on the four lanky band members. Though he doubted he was *that* much older than them, he couldn't help seeing them as kids, still filled with the ignorance of youth, hoping to make it big someday, like it'd make all their dreams come true. Good to know what a bitter old fuck he'd become at the ripe age of twenty-eight.

As Infamous Goat went into their first song, he snuck a glance at Claire. The profile picture hadn't done her justice. What he'd seen as beauty in the photo paled in comparison to the woman in front of him. In the low light, her hair looked black, highlighting her creamy skin, and her eyes still shone the same striking blue. Maybe she wore contacts? No, he doubted it. He refused to believe anything about her could be artificial.

She gestured toward the band. "They're not bad."

"No, they're not. Their lead guy's vocals need some refinement, but he's got potential. Good riffs. Solid bass work. And that drummer kicks serious ass."

Kind of like Dejected when it started out. And being with Jocelyn had taken his songwriting to a whole new level, one he wasn't sure he could have achieved without her. "Beautiful Blaze" had been his crown jewel.

The riff he'd worked on earlier still resounded in his head though, and the more time he spent on the date, the stronger it got, until it took over his entire subconscious, pushing out his ex, his resentment, and his fear. The way it should be.

Grabbing one of the napkins, he took a pen out of his pocket and jotted down a couple of lines, started something new, not tainted by Joss or by Sleeping Angels. His alone.

When the band finished, Claire clapped and whooped, reminding him of the glory days before everything fell apart, when Dejected had played places like this and their dreams of stardom still meant being *together*. That one random drunk person would clap and whoop louder than any of their fans and friends. He missed those days. Right then, he even missed Anderson. For that, he blamed the alcohol.

He swigged the last of his drink and hoped Infamous Goat never made it further than this bar. The real world had teeth and claws that idealistic little bastards like them knew nothing about.

As the group went into a hard rock cover, Claire scooted her chair closer to his, leaving no space between them. At that point, he'd had enough liquid courage to place his hand on her thigh. She rested her head on his shoulder for a moment then placed a quick kiss on his cheek before turning her attention back to the band and lightly singing along.

Without a second thought, he wrapped an arm around her. He wanted her close.

The band ended the song and, just when he thought leaving for the hotel was a good idea, the lead singer looked square at *him*. "Holy shit! Is that Ty Krause?"

The entire crowd turned to stare. He offered a half-smile and prayed he wouldn't hear what he knew would come next.

"Man, we love Dejected. Come up here!"

"Yeah," Claire said in his ear. "Go on up, rock star." The sound of her voice sent ripples through him. In that tone, he'd do anything she asked.

To claps and cheers—most of them from her—he did as requested. The familiar strains of "The Song" filled the bar. God. Fucking. Damn it.

The sound wasn't as tight as he liked, but apparently, Infamous Goat had played it more than a few times, probably to get laid at prom. He grabbed the mic, unused to being onstage without his bass, and let go.

I couldn't explain if I tried a thousand years
And searched through every word in existence, baby
But your love, it boils and burns and sears

Ignites and scorches, leaves me defenseless, baby.
A million lifetimes, or this one I'm living
I'll live it all in this love you're giving.

As the music swelled toward the chorus, he looked over at his beautiful wordsmith, who sang along, seemingly entranced. And, for some reason, he loved watching her.

And we're just learnin', burnin'
Flames and embers
Baby, watch it flicker
Leaving me yearnin'
And you know the fumes—they consume
Fire so ashen
Drenched in passion
And it burns right through
This second, this moment, all these days
It's a beautiful blaze.

The entire bar sang along, and rather than the disdain he usually experienced, he buzzed with the electricity in the air, and the second verse became Claire's and hers alone.

Can't shake how shaken you're making me feel
Like you're pouring me full of kerosene, baby
Every touch, what a blaze it'll kindle
Blistering dance that is so serene, baby.

This time, the crowd sang the chorus for him. He held out the microphone, but he only cared about her. Her eyes closed and her mouth formed the words, and he started loving this song again, but for a different reason.

It was becoming his truth. For her.

Don't wanna ever let this blaze burn low
Wanna see how long this fire will glow.
And we're just learnin', burnin'
Flames and embers
Baby, watch it flicker
Leaving me yearnin'
And you know the fumes—they consume
Fire so ashen
Drenched in passion
And it burns right through
This second, this moment, all these days
It's a beautiful blaze.

Chills ran through Claire the moment Ty opened his mouth. Trepidation echoed in his voice, and heartbreak, but as he continued, he grew more confident in the lyrics until, by the end, he sounded triumphant, leading the crowd in a fevered sing-along. However, none of it compared to the way he looked at her. Sexy, hopeful. *Ready.*

When the music stopped, uproarious cheers erupted, and hers were the loudest, though she doubted he'd hear. After jumping off stage, high-fiving a few of the patrons, he beelined to her, enveloping her in his arms, and crushed his mouth to hers. The intensity in it demanded she yield, and she did without any other thought, letting him dominate her while relishing every second. With her body pressed tight to his, she couldn't imagine being elsewhere and had never been so grateful to her heart for overriding her mind and preventing her from walking out the door.

In a matter of minutes, they were back in the Castillo Hotel, Downtown Charleston, fumbling for keycards, still kissing and nipping whatever they could touch. Finally managing to get the door open, they spilled inside in a tangle of limbs, tugging at clothing. Since thinking had become overrated, she operated purely on instinct and feeling, not at all concerned that a few hours earlier the man had been a stranger, and now he was the closest thing to a lover she'd had in almost half a decade.

The door slammed behind them, and he pushed her against it, pinning her with his hard body. Animal lust sparkled in his dark eyes, the same lust coursing through her. His song played in her mind while he maneuvered her panties down her legs. So close to him, she inhaled the cologne lingering on his neck and the underlying scent of pure male that, both scents together, created an irresistible concoction.

"Please," she whispered, barely able to hear her voice above her racing heart.

After another quick nip to her neck, he pulled away long enough to dig around in his pocket, his knuckles brushing her thigh. He undid his trousers, fiddled with the condom he'd fished out, sheathed his cock, then lifted her. With her legs around his waist, she was almost breathless with anticipation. *Five years*. Five long, horrible, unsatisfying years spent with characters having way more sex than their author.

He rammed inside her with desperation. A loud groan built in her throat, a mix of the pain and pleasure causing her vision to blur. Shutting her eyes, she concentrated on his thrusts and the sweet pressure building in her core. She clawed his shoulders, wishing to rip off the fabric still covering him, eager for skin-to-skin contact.

His scruffy cheek brushed her neck, his hot breath puffing on the sensitive area. For once, she truly understood what her characters experienced in all those steamy scenes she'd written. She hadn't been doing them justice, but at that point, her confidence in her ability to appropriately convey the connection of two souls didn't exist. Every time he moved, euphoria threatened to steal her breath. The closer she came to climax, the more aware she grew of every touch, ragged breath, and needful sound her rock star made. She fought the rising tide, desperate to prolong their connection, have more time to enjoy it, but she simply couldn't. With her body trapped between him and the unforgiving wooden door, she gave in to her need, and the last five years evaporated.

After a couple more pumps, Ty came with a hoarse grunt, shivers wracking his entire body. Claire wiped his hair from his sweat-sheened face while he struggled to catch his breath. With a smile on his swollen lips, he lowered her to the floor, but before she could speak, he covered her mouth with his and she opened to him.

She hadn't been kissed like that...ever. Certainly not by Neil, who had won the Wet Dishrag award several years running. The tide of desire rolled over her again, but Ty backed away before she drowned and pressed his forehead to hers.

"Definitely not the way I'd planned that."

"I'm not complaining." She chuckled.

Jesus H. Christ. He already wanted round two with Miss Romance Author. He'd sworn off quickies, but with the way she'd looked at him in the bar, he'd had to have her the second they were anywhere near privacy. And how she looked at him right now, round two was not far away.

Taking her hand, he led her to the dinette and pretended he could still be a gentleman in her presence by pulling out her chair. Then he headed to the mini-fridge and grabbed a couple of beers. He offered her the longneck. Her disheveled look killed him in the best fucking way. Still eyeballing him, she wrapped her lips around it and took a deep gulp, a smile tugging at the corners of her mouth. *If there's a God, her mouth will be doing that to my cock later.*

"Mind if I ask a question?"

"Sure thing." He'd tell her whatever she wanted.

"Why music?"

He grinned. "Why writing?"

Understanding softened her face. "Touché, rock star."

"Seriously, though, if you want an answer...it's pretty much all I've ever been good at. I didn't go to college. Went straight for my dream." He shrugged with what he hoped was nonchalance. Claire was smart as fuck, so admitting he'd never done the college thing made him feel about three inches tall.

"I respect that. Trust me, you didn't miss much, except maybe a few keggers at frat houses and a ton of student loans afterward." Despite the casual conversation, desire swam in the ocean of her gorgeous eyes. "And between you and me, you made the right choice."

"Glad you think so. Sleeping Angels isn't complaining."

"What is the name of that song...'Something-Summer'?"

"'Seize the Summer.'" He took a swig. "I still can't believe I wrote that shit. I think I was drunk at the time. Or maybe it came from *Mad Libs*. Either way, alcohol was involved."

She laughed, the real, genuine laugh captured in her profile photo. Briefly, he recalled his mission to hear the sound that came with the smile. *Mission accomplished.*

"It's...catchy?"

"Catchy is all it takes these days."

"It sells. Sometimes you have to put aside your true dreams to pay the bills," she said.

Interesting.... "So romance wasn't your first choice?"

"Nope. It kind of happened. I love it—don't get me wrong—but my first love, my true love, is science fiction."

"Like *Star Trek* science fiction?"

"*Star Trek, Jurassic Park, Star Wars, Firefly.* Whatever my brain can fit itself around. I love it. I love all the potential." As she spoke, her face lit with the same passion he felt for music. "It's just too bad I'm better at romance."

He never would have pegged her as a hardcore sci-fi lover. Should have figured when she'd said her favorite Bruce Willis movies were *The Fifth Element* and *Surrogates*. No one ever picked those. He caught himself before asking about the research she did. Instead, he asked, "You could combine the two, right?"

The sparkle in her eyes dimmed. "I threw a few science fiction elements into my last series, but it didn't work. My ideas never had romance in them. I feel like it always falls flat. Someday, maybe I'll get back to it. Right now, I'm having fun with the romances. I love my *Chicagoland Chronicles* series."

Ty lifted his drink. She stared at him like he'd lost his damn mind until he said the only thing he remembered from any English class. "How about a toast to dreams deferred?"

Note to self. English references work like magic on sexy authors. Claire had chugged the last bit of her beer, placed the bottle on the table, and grabbed his tie, using it as a leash. Destination? The bed. He couldn't wipe the shit-eating grin off his face. Round two was *on*.

Still holding onto the makeshift lead, she maneuvered him onto the oversized bed, clutching the tie as she straddled him, like he'd go anywhere else. He liked the playfulness, though. Seeing that side of his demure date turned him on, almost as much as her plea of, "Fuck me." Blood rushed south at the thought of doing just that.

He threaded his fingers through her dark hair and brought her mouth to his. But, this time, he intended to slow it down, touch, tease, and taste every part of her, the way he'd planned, but failed, before taking her against the door. While hot, it hadn't given him the same satisfaction that this would.

Plus, she wore nothing under her dress. His mouth watered thinking about it, and his cock saluted. After unzipping the dress and pulling it down her torso, he coaxed her onto her back. He wanted her completely naked. *Now*.

Slipping the fabric the rest of the way down her legs, he prayed he'd hold off long enough to give her the experience she deserved because all he wanted to do was insert tab A into slot B. Over and over. He'd have to stay clothed, though. Otherwise, it would last as long as the door sex. Not long enough.

"Damn," he said. His version of perfection lay naked beneath him. Soft curves, supple skin, not one of those bony chicks who had always thrown themselves at him after shows. He still couldn't figure out how men found that attractive. Settling between his wordsmith's thighs, he covered her body with his, then kissed her again, unable to get enough of her sweet lips.

She smiled. "You're wearing too much."

"There's a reason for that." His lips hovered above hers. "If I take off my clothes, I'll have to fuck you."

A larger grin spread across her face. "How awful for you," she teased.

"Terrible." He nibbled her jaw and cupped one of her breasts, running the pad of his thumb across the hard nipple. "Horrible, even. You're the author. You come up with the right words."

"Mmm." She tangled a hand in his hair. "Right now I don't even want to think."

"Good." He took in the view of the beautiful woman laid out before him, tamping down the desire to flip her onto her stomach and fuck her like an animal. Though the fantasy, with Nine Inch Nails', "Closer" playing in the background almost had him busting a nut. *That* would have been embarrassing.

Instead, he tried to keep it like slow jazz, seductive and enticing, but with the absolute 100-proof lust flowing through his body, he had no idea how long it'd be before he surrendered to his inner Trent Reznor.

Judging by the way her nails raked his skin and the noises she made at every touch, it wouldn't be much longer. Almost desperate to hear her beg, Ty waited for the magic words. She would beg. And she'd love it when he gave in. In theory, he could hold out. *Concentrate on her, dumbass.* Taking in the view again, he decided he could definitely do that.

She squirmed beneath him, urging him between her legs. He stroked her inner thigh to her swollen pussy lips, watched the look in her eyes grow more intense. Sensual. Without taking his gaze from hers, he spread her and covered her clit with his mouth. No warming her up—no need.

This woman. Goddamn. He could get addicted to the sounds she made, the way she tasted, how her body moved in response to pleasure. As he slipped two fingers inside her soaked entrance, she bucked. More than ready, more than willing. *Say it, Claire. Come on.*

Still nothing but the sexiest moans he'd heard in a long time. The more aroused she became, the huskier her voice grew. She ground against him, and he sucked her clit between his teeth, flicking his tongue along the sensitive tip. Her back arched and her hips jolted, inner walls putting a stranglehold on his fingers. He kept stroking and sucking, determined to make her see stars. It became a game to him, one they'd both win, and only a matter of time to see who could hold out the longest.

Right then, he was the victor, but not by much. His pants had a death grip on his cock and he'd have to take them off soon.

But.... Abandoning her clit, he concentrated on finger-fucking her. She was so close to coming, and he got so *hot* watching her. The raw sensuality forced the temperature in the room to skyrocket. With a shudder and a hoarse cry, she climaxed, and he couldn't take his eyes off her. Had never seen anything as exquisite as his beautiful wordsmith. Even Dejected's last show didn't compare to the joy of knowing how much he pleasured the amazing woman.

After catching her breath, she reached for him, and he went to her, his hunger reaching critical mass. Almost in a daze, he shed his clothes, focused only on Claire, feeling her flushed skin against his. Like he'd wanted to do from the start, he flipped her onto her stomach and tugged her hips up. *Shit*. His pants had ended up on the other side of the bed somewhere.

"Hold that thought, babe." Bounding off the bed, he located his trousers then grabbed another condom from the pocket. Once sufficiently covered, he turned back to a jaw-dropping sight. Ass still in the air, Claire stroked her clit while she waited for him, watching him, her mouth curved in a seductive grin. *Who is this woman?* He would never have expected such wantonness from the woman he'd met in the restaurant downstairs. His cock spasmed as if reminding him to hurry. No more waiting.

He slipped inside her, and the experience was like the Christmas morning so many years ago when he'd unwrapped his first guitar—relief that he'd gotten what he'd asked for, along with total satisfaction. Grasping her hips, he slammed her again and again. Then needing a different angle, he grabbed her neck and pushed her head to the pillows. She canted her hips and the slight tilt made all the difference for them both. Her inner muscles clamped around his cock and he rode her through another orgasm, wondering if he could make her come one more time before his own release.

He did, then he gave in, needing the release more than ever. And *fuck*, it felt better than it ever had.

"Claire," he whispered, her name like a prayer on his lips. Begrudgingly, he pulled out of her and removed the condom. Man, he needed to clean up before he even thought about touching her again. She stretched like a cat then curled onto her side. After a quick kiss, he headed to the bathroom. When he slid next to her a couple minutes later, she'd already fallen asleep, a sated smile on her face.

***

Claire rolled onto her back, cursing her small bladder. She hadn't had much to drink, only the bourbon and Coke, and one beer, yet her body demanded she rise at the ungodly hour of...she glanced at the clock...4:47 a.m.

And she was alone.

Tossing off the covers, she scanned the floor for her clothes, but her tired eyes failed her in the dark. Instead, she grabbed Ty's shirt—the closest thing she found—and slipped it on, taking time to button it to her waist, for no other reason than modesty, strange since she'd completely abandoned it earlier.

He'd supposedly shut his phone off. If he'd

turned it on, left her there in favor of his stupid-ass ex.... What would Claire do? What *could* she do? He and Joss had a history she had no chance against. Besides, she and Ty had one night. Not like they would last beyond the hotel room door, regardless of the dozens of testimonials she'd read on the 1Night Stand website declaring soul mates and all that other bull. Even as a romance author, she didn't believe in that anymore.

Also, where the everloving hell was the bathroom? In the dark, the room might as well have been a cave. She couldn't make out any of the shapes of the furniture and nearly walked into the couch before sounds coming from the balcony registered. Music. And a certain rock star's soft voice working through lyrics. *Wow. Way to overreact.*

Shaking her head, she continued feeling her way across the room. Maybe they had hope after all. Maybe a failed science-fiction writer and a former hard rock god could chase their dreams together.

Chapter Five

Ty wracked his brain to find the right words. What he'd written in his head at the bar turned out to be the bridge, and the rest eluded him, though the melody played a loop in his brain. Awesome. A melody, a bridge, and uncooperative verses and chorus.

For once, he had too many ideas. Writing "The Song" hadn't been this difficult. Of course, that had been penned by a boy with a boy's thoughts and desires. The new song demanded far more from him.

Plus the damn guitar app on his phone sucked balls.

He'd drawn bars and staff on hotel stationary and tried to fill in lyrics and notes, but between the lyrics fighting every step of the way and the mild headache the app gave him, he hadn't gotten far, spending more time cursing the stupid phone under his breath than actually working.

"Thought you could use this."

He jumped. Claire laughed lightly behind him and handed him a glass of water. Quickly, he covered the page; not because he refused to let someone see a project until he had finished it—in fact, he probably could have used her vocabulary—but because it belonged to her.

She deserved something like that. Unknowingly, she'd changed everything for him by being herself. Maybe someday he'd write something for himself again. Maybe not.

"What are you doing out here?" she asked. And she was wearing his shirt? Not that he would complain. She wore it better than he did.

He shrugged, trying to stay cool and collected, wanting to surprise her with the finished product. "Working on some music. Didn't want to wake you." Her lazy smile warmed him, made his heart beat faster. Leaning toward her, he fingered a strand of her silky hair. "Go to bed. I'll be there soon."

Nodding, she kissed him with more passion than he'd expected. "Don't keep me waiting too long, rock star."

"Wouldn't dream of it, wordsmith." He sent her back in with a playful swat on the ass. "And ditch my shirt. You look too good in it."

In response, she threw it on his head.

If the muses hadn't been singing so loudly, he would've followed her in and capitalized on the little game, but he had a song to finish. Once she heard it, she'd understand.

It might be his best one yet.

***

Daylight had crept through the trees and above the buildings before he finally packed in the phone and notepad, the latter ending up in his overnight bag. Still zonked out, Claire had the covers pooled around her waist. For a few seconds, he stood and watched her, taking in every inch of exposed skin, then disrobed and joined her, placing the phone on the nightstand as he always did. He lightly pressed his lips to her shoulder before shifting her hair from her neck and nibbling on the skin. A breathy moan hit him straight in the cock, and she rolled onto her side, her sleepy, sexy grin getting him to half-mast with no effort at all. He hungered for her like a man on death row looking forward to his last meal.

Dinnertime.

He kissed her, slowly, sensually, but all pretense of legitimate lovemaking crumbled when she gripped his erection. She pushed his shoulder, and he obliged her by rolling onto his back.

Shedding the covers, she straddled him, and in the early dawn light, he made out the silhouette of her body, the curve of her breasts, and the waves of dark hair cascading down her body and brushing his stomach like fine strands of silk. Goddess, angel, everything. She eased down to lap the head of his cock. When she took more of the shaft into her mouth, his body clenched. And the pressure, sweet God, the pressure while she sucked him off was just as intense as being inside her. How the hell had he ever thought he'd be able to let her walk out of his life in a few hours?

Claire caressing his balls brought him to the here-and-now. He couldn't let her go. He wouldn't. Fuck that shit. "God, Claire." She purred in the back of her throat, and the vibrations almost killed him. "Babe, I'm gonna come."

As he did, she sucked harder. *Is that even*

possible? She swallowed everything he had like a champ then kissed him. After a cat-like stretch, she curled next to him, head resting on his chest. "I don't want this to end, rock star," she said, sleepiness coating her voice and slurring her words.

"Me neither, wordsmith." *Maybe it doesn't have to.*

***

The all-too-familiar strains of "Cold Hard Bitch" intruded on an amazing dream about Claire and the private beach behind his house. Without thinking, he grabbed his phone. The voice on the other end of the line took him by surprise, even if he should have expected it.

"I'm here all alone and I need you."

Something about that statement didn't sit well with him. Why wouldn't she be lonely? Anderson's band was playing in Prague and she didn't go on tour with them. *Duh, Joss.*

"Not my problem," he mumbled and hung up.

Just as he began to doze, the phone rang again. *Fucking A.* If he didn't deal with her, she'd keep calling. And calling. And calling.

Answering again, he said, "I'm coming," and hung up. *Time to end this.*

Claire hoped she'd only dreamed Ty's phone rang, but her fears were confirmed when she woke to an empty bed. *Really? I should've figured.*

On autopilot, she gathered her clothes, dressed, and made sure she left with everything she'd entered with. Aside, of course, from dignity. It'd take a while before she had that again.

She stopped at the door. Unfortunately, she couldn't let this go. She and Ty had a connection; she knew it with everything in her, but they wouldn't have a chance to let it flourish thanks to that bitch, Joss. Glancing around, Claire searched for the stationary she'd spotted earlier on the nightstand, but it was no longer there. Fine. She'd use her own pen and paper to get the thoughts out of her head.

Logically, she understood Neil and his cheating had caused the ferocious ache in her chest, and Ty was not Neil. Her mangled relationship with her previous lover had led to her writing romance and searching for a way to make sense of it all, to learn the inner workings of love and what made people return to those who'd hurt them. In the five years since their breakup, she'd gained more knowledge than she anticipated, talked with readers and fans for whom her characters' relationships had proven helpful with their own difficult situations, and yet, she had never quite put the past behind her.

She'd start that day. By doing what she hadn't done with Neil—letting Ty know exactly how much she hurt.

Settling on the sofa, legs tucked under her, she searched through her purse for the small notebook she always kept. To waste words and time on the situation rankled her beyond belief, but, damn it, she'd hated waking up alone and he needed to know that.

At least Trace and Ella still wanted her. She had plenty of work to do on their story when she got home.

First, she had a note to write.

Dear Ty. No. That wouldn't work. She ripped the page out and crumpled it up.

Ty—

I'm sure I know exactly where you are, and to say I'm disappointed is an understatement.

She crossed that out. Sounded too much like an angry parent. Taking a deep breath, she tried one more time.

Ty—

I wish you'd been here when I woke up. After everything we've shared, the empty bed was an insult. Maybe you're too scared to move on from her. I can understand that, but you acted like you wanted more with me. I wanted more. As long as she's in your life, though, there's no room for me.

I hope you find something akin to happiness with her.

Claire

There. Short and sweet.

For the next hour, she'd give Penny a piece of her mind, then *maybe* try to better her mood with *All Roads Lead to You*. Or write in a different genre altogether. No more romance. Ever.

Of course, the rational part of her mind told her she overreacted. One fantastic-then-failed date didn't mean she'd chosen an incorrect career or life path. Today simply wasn't her day. The pissed-off part decided it'd had enough and wanted to settle in with a bowl of ice cream and a Bruce Willis marathon.

Once she got to her car, she dialed Penelope. *Please pick up. Please, please, please pick up.*

Before voice-mail kicked in, Penny answered. "Please tell me it was amazing and the best thing ever, and that you're gonna have his babies."

Claire sighed. "I'm telling you none of that."

She practically heard Penny's shoulders sag through the phone. For the next several miles, she told the entire story, beginning to end, with as much detail as she could remember. "So whatever testimonials you read on the website, I won't be adding to them."

A few moments of silence passed. She weaved in and out of traffic, eager to get home and into the loving arms of John McClane. *Die Hard* made everything better, even the one with Justin Long and Kevin Smith. No ex-girlfriends to worry about.

"I'm sorry."

"It's fine. I have work to do. *Roads* is almost finished." Then the *Chicagoland Chronicles* would be, too.

"Fair enough. I'm already planning your release party."

This I have to hear.

"You know that sweet bookstore on Illinois Street that was *always* booked up when we tried to get it?" Penny asked.

No way, no way, no way. "Yeeeeah...?"

"Well, I wanted to surprise you with the news, but since I signed you up for that shitty date and all...I got the store booked for your *Roads* release. As long as you finish it on time, that is."

They'd been trying to book an event at Penman's Progress for *years*. So many amazing authors had signed there. "I'm not worthy."

"I know. And, to put some more icing on this delicious cake, I booked you the best Chicago cover band in...well, in Chicago. We're sending this series off with a bang, my dear."

"All is forgiven. You are my fairy godmother. Remind me to buy you a wand."

"I'd rather have a sword."

"You can have whatever your heart desires."

"Right now, I'd like to have the knowledge that your editor has your book. So get home and finish that. Then we'll discuss my heart's desires."

"Your wish is my command."

Chapter Six

Seven months later

Claire had forgotten how cold Chicago could be in the winter, but having a third-quarter release meant braving the Windy City's cutting wind. She shivered even after reaching shelter, but having access to her favorite bookstore in the entire country made the chill insignificant. She'd loved Penman's Progress since her first visit six years earlier, when she'd been celebrating her first *Chicagoland Chronicles* book, *Come in from the Night*. Walking the streets with Neil, she'd gone in, fallen in love, and declared that someday, she'd have a signing there.

Climbing the staircase—with a lovely wrought iron railing—up to the second floor, she couldn't believe the day had finally arrived. On the landing, she stopped for a moment before heading to the table to prepare, savoring the feel of the ornate, cool metal under her palm. *Oh, yeah.* Definitely adding some of that to the house. She didn't have a second floor, but she'd find a way. Maybe she could redo the porch.

Penny greeted her with a bright smile and a bruising hug. "What do you think?" She gestured around the room.

Turning to take it all in, Claire inhaled the scent of books, both new and old. Exposed brick and beautiful vintage lampposts decorated the room. From that floor, the windows faced Lake Michigan, offering a gorgeous, albeit frosty, view of the water. Enough merchandise to choke a horse covered the table, and a large portrait of *Roads'* cover, with Ella and Trace in all their 1920s glory, sat on an easel next to it. Behind it, the staff had placed shelves containing the other four books in the series. Three rows of chairs to accommodate guests sat directly in front of the table. Against the far wall, a stage had been set up where the band, 25 or 6 to 4, would start playing after her reading and signing concluded—provided they showed up on time. A childlike giddiness flooded her. Everything she'd ever dreamed of surrounded her.

Except for the missing piece.

She'd regretted not leaving some sort of contact information for Ty, but had left so angry, the idea hadn't crossed her mind. Once she'd gotten home and poured herself a glass of wine, she'd planted her butt in the chair and started the long process of polishing the last twenty-four thousand words of Ella and Trace's story, from the dance, to the high-speed chase on the back roads between Chicago and Des Plaines, to the couple's eventual reunion. She'd never thought she could make a romance between a policeman's daughter and a bootlegger work, but it'd somehow happened, and her editor had loved it. The process flew by, leaving her brain too occupied or too exhausted to think about the failed date. Until she had no more book to work on. No edits, no cover design discussions, nothing. Then, thoughts of Ty and the irritating idea of what could have been, returned.

Rather than go down that road, she'd dusted off the old science fiction novel she'd dreamed of publishing, started ripping it apart, and dedicated all of her energy to it. Before catching her flight that morning, she'd completed a rough draft. A *much* better rough draft, thus answering at least one question of what could have been. The other would remain a mystery.

"It's perfect," she replied. "Better than I could have imagined."

"Good. It was hell to put together," Penny said with a wink. "Now, we're going to have an introduction, the reading, and a quick Q&A before the signing. Then the party starts."

Book signings never got easier for Claire, and readings even less so. She took a decent pull of whisky from the flask her friend had so kindly provided and reviewed the section in the book she'd highlighted for the reading. Looking over the familiar words, she smiled. She loved this part.

People started filing into the room, and her jitters kicked into high gear. Penny flitted around like the good hostess Claire wasn't, offering the coffee and tea Penman's Progress had provided and directing readers to the seats. In the meantime, she exchanged pleasantries and forced her lunch to stay where she'd put it. The brief calm her shot of whiskey brought no longer existed.

Everyone settled, and a roomful of gazes turned

to her. Now in the spotlight, she had to turn on her author charm. Hopefully, she hadn't left the on switch at home.

"Thank y'all for coming," she said. Her southern accent always sounded so much worse to her ears in the North. "I'm so happy to see some familiar faces and some new ones as well. The *Chicagoland Chronicles* series is one of my most favorites, and I'm thrilled to share the celebration of *All Roads Lead to You* with you all."

Truth be told, she loved her readers. They were some of the best and most loyal in the world. "This last book of the series embodies the upheaval of the Prohibition era in the relationship of its central characters, Ella Maas, the daughter of a corrupt Chicago policeman, and Trace Bishop, a down-and-out kid who turns to bootlegging to make his fortune."

The gasps and claps from the crowd invigorated her. Though her nerves still hadn't calmed, she thought she'd be able to make it through the reading, even if it this part reminded her most of Ty.

"The selection I wanted to read is the first time the two see each other, which happens at a speakeasy. Of course." Cue the chuckles. Such a good audience. "Ella's out with her girlfriends, without a chaperone. They end up at the speakeasy where Trace is...enjoying some of the finer perks of being in Al Capone's employ." She took a deep breath and began to read, praying she wouldn't sound like a complete idiot.

Trace took a deep swig of the whiskey, savoring the burn in the back of his throat. He'd taken it all the way from Atlantic City to Chicago, his first big job for Scarface, and now he was sitting pretty with the promise of moving up in the gang. Running provided excitement, but he wanted more responsibility. A way to prove his old man wrong once and for all.

Nutsy elbowed him in the side, a wide grin overrunning his narrow face. Kid had a face like a rat, but everybody said he was nuttier than a bushel of acorns, hence the nickname. "Look at them skirts in the corner," he said.

Following the kid's line of vision, Trace looked, and his heart stopped. Working with Capone, he'd seen his fair share of gorgeous broads, but she...she was a goddess. Clara Bow had nothing on her.

"Damn, look at the gams on that one."

Nutsy gestured to the blonde, the one making him dizzy. She had legs up to her neck, long, toned, like a dancer's. Licking his lips, he imagined how those legs would feel wrapped around his waist.

Lame-foot Larraby sat on his other side, blocking his view. "Her?" He snorted. "Her and those girls are high hats, man. Too ritzy for bums like you. Besides, a lot of these flapper dames are flat tires. All looks, no brains."

"I'm gonna go talk to her." What did he have to lose?

With an unsubtle shake of his head, Lame-foot tsked. "You'll go over one of the best and brightest and come back public enemy number one with them dames. Just wait, pal."

"Hey, maybe he'll get her name," Nutsy said. "Then maybe he can teach you to dance the Charleston!"

The two men howled with laughter. Trace drained his whiskey, stood up, and smoothed his shirt. "You guys are a coupla boobs, you know that?"

They laughed harder.

He'd show 'em. First, he'd make himself Capone's best runner. Then he'd nab a slew of chicks like these. Starting with her.

The trio turned at his approach. The two friends looked him up and down. She, though, met his eyes and smiled, showing white teeth behind painted red lips. He thanked his lucky stars she couldn't see how nervous he was.

"Havin' a good time, ladies?"

"Yeah," the blonde answered. "This place is great."

Trace detected a hint of sarcasm in the girl's honey-sweet voice, like she didn't want to be there after all. The other two didn't say a word, but both looked like the cat that swallowed the canary.

Had he missed something?

With a conspiratorial grin, Claire closed the book to some *ooohs* from the crowd. Once the party got into full swing, she grew more at ease, fielding questions like a pro. Then she settled into the chair and relaxed through the signing, peeking up every so often to check for the missing band.

The strains of an acoustic guitar didn't escape her notice. Head buried in book after book, she figured the band's guitarist was just practicing. When she looked up though, her heart jolted. In the entryway, decked out in a tight black sweater and carpenter jeans, stood her rock star, acoustic guitar in his hands. He cleared his throat, and every eye in the room turned to him.

That was *not* the way he'd intended to reunite with Claire, but desperate times and all that shit. He hated crashing her party. More than that, he'd hated how everything had ended so abruptly between them, without an opportunity to explain.

Yeah, he'd left without telling her, and it had been a stupid mistake. After all, he'd intended to try for a second date. Then a third. Then a fourth.... He'd wanted more. But, unlike her, he hadn't been smart enough to leave a note. He'd had to deal with his ex, and Claire'd given him the courage to do that.

With Joss out of his life, he concentrated on music, most notably the song that had consumed him at the Castillo in Charleston. Every part of it had to be perfect so she'd understand. He always made a mess of verbal communication, but in a song, he could tell her exactly how he felt.

Seeing her so happy almost made him lose his nerve. He thought about her note every day, how she'd said she wanted more, how he'd definitely wanted more. If this last-ditch effort blew up in his face, he'd never live it down.

When she spotted him, her expression spoke volumes and steeled his resolve. Her eyes were as big as plates, mouth slightly open. Not angry, maybe stunned. Stepping forward, he played through the intro again, hoping to come in with the lyrics that time. Thank God everyone had stopped talking; he'd never be able to project over the noise.

You're no addiction
If you were I could quit you

And I couldn't leave you even if I tried
It's all dependence
A need I've sunk into
Dazed and craving, safe and satisfied
Stuck in the past, in my own misery
'Til you held out a hand and saved me from me.

She stared at him in bewilderment, as though she couldn't believe he'd shown up. Part of him couldn't either. He'd planned for months, stalking her website to find out where she'd be and when. Her release party had given him the best chance to make up to her. And since the band she'd booked was apparently running late....

You didn't give me the strength to stand and fight
You are my strength, every single part
You didn't mend what was broken inside
How could you fix it when you are my heart
You didn't give me a reason to let it go
You're my living reason to live and be
You completed my want, my need, and so
For eternity—Complete Me.

In his mind, he begged her not to be angry. He'd spent their time apart perfecting the song, grateful for Sleeping Angels' extended tour and break from recording. The little bastards were back at school in Britain, and far away from him. All he'd wanted sat in front of him, her sparkling eyes rimmed with tears.

My head's site of healing
My soul's source of comfort

My love's never-ending spot of contentment
My future revealed and
My love discovered
Staring in the eyes of my new beginning.
My heart's true hero, my one cause for each dream
The breath that's stolen when you can't help but gleam.

Yeah, he'd read her *Chicagoland Chronicles* series and her previous sci-fi series, and all of her blog posts to hear her voice in his mind. He'd missed her so much his soul ached. For seven long months, he'd absorbed all things Claire, but it had been a teaspoon of water to a parched man's lips. She stood in front of him then, a smile of disbelief on her perfect lips. He went into the chorus again, then into the last bridge, the one that had been hardest to write because it encapsulated everything he'd felt without her.

Had you in my arms, your caress, your kiss
There's no other love to compare to this.

She had to know. He'd fallen head over heels for her in one night, and he'd give anything to have her in his arms every morning from there on out. After playing a small interlude, he sang the chorus with all the conviction he could muster.

You didn't give me the strength to stand and fight
You are my strength, every single part
You didn't mend what was broken inside

How could you fix it when you are my heart
You didn't give me a reason to let it go
You're my living reason to live and be
You completed my want, my need, and so
For eternity—Complete Me.

The last notes faded and he and Claire stared at each other, inches apart. Ty gingerly placed the guitar to the side, never breaking eye contact. He waited for her reaction, almost expecting her to scream at him, slap him, anything, never imagining what happened next.

Around them, the crowd started to clap. She closed the distance and he mentally prepared for her reaction, whatever it might be. When she pounced on him, he almost lost his balance, but held her steady and answered her claiming kiss with the pent-up longing and desire he'd carried for so many months. The room erupted with cheers.

Being in Ty's arms again...she'd needed him the entire time. Crowd of onlookers be damned, she'd show him how much she'd missed him.

But too much longer, and her readers would get a show they hadn't intended to see. Hesitantly, she broke the kiss. "You owe me an explanation."

He got a kicked-puppy look. "I know. I'm so sorry, Claire. Can we go somewhere and talk?"

"Yeah. After I get this done, you're all mine."

She signed like the wind, all the while casting brief glances at her rock star while he chatted with Penny. Because that was a *great* idea. Once the event drew to a close, she grabbed Ty and half-dragged him out of the bookstore. Down the street sat a great coffee shop where they could talk without interruption.

After they were seated and had their drinks, she couldn't think of what she wanted to say. Over the months, she'd played and replayed conversations in her mind—one of them had actually made it into her current work-in-progress—but as she sat there, her brain shut down.

Thank goodness he started the conversation. "I fucked up. So hard."

She laughed. "Yes. You did. But you're here." It still didn't seem real. "What happened?"

Shaking his head, he stared down at his coffee cup. "I thought I'd be back before you woke up."

For the first time, her high diminished. *Do I really want to hear this?*

"Joss called. Said she was lonely. She...she'd do that from time to time when Anderson, her boyfriend, the guy she left me for, would go on tour with his band. And I'd always answer because I didn't know what else to do. I never had anything worth giving her up for. Until you." He stopped. Their eyes met and she saw the uncertainty in his.

Covering his hand with hers, she smiled her reassurance. "Keep going."

With a sigh of relief, he did. "I've driven to her house so many times I could do it in my sleep. I moved to New York to get away from her, but every summer, I hole up in a little beach house on Kiawah Island where I can work. And where I can still be close to her.

"We—we had this down to an art, to the point that she knew how long it'd take me to get to her place from my beach house. When it didn't take half as long for me to arrive as she thought it should, she started screaming at me. I told her I'd found someone, I was happy, and that if she didn't leave me the fuck alone, I'd tell Anderson everything." He shrugged. "Not one of my finer moments."

Claire's heart thundered in her ears. "So it's finished? No more Joss? No calls?"

"She doesn't have a chance. I've changed every bit of my contact info. The only people who have my phone number are my mom and Sleeping Angels' manager." Shifting in his seat, he leaned forward. "I would have gotten to the room by nine a.m. if there hadn't been a wreck on the interstate, in one of those spots where I couldn't get a signal to save my life. I think I cussed enough to make a sailor with Tourette's blush."

"Ty...." Damn it, tears again. With his free hand, he wiped them from her cheeks. She said, "I was so wrong."

"Li'l bit." He laughed with her that time. "I wanted to get that shit done, then get to you, tell you the good news. I should have let you know." After a brief pause, he said, "Then maybe we could have been spending the last seven months together instead of...well, not."

"How about I make it up to you then?"

He cocked an eyebrow. That piqued his interest. "I won't complain."

Perfect. "As it turns out, I've started writing a series that requires some original songs. It's not the same as—"

"Done. Whatever you want, whatever you need. Done."

"I'll pay you for your help."

"Will work for sex," he said with a grin.

"Good, because that's how I intend to pay you." Warmth cascaded through her at the thought. She'd fantasized about him too often not to blush. "I've missed you."

"I missed you, too, babe. More than you know."

"Enough to write me a song?" she teased.

"Yeah, well, we have to play to our strengths, right?"

"Right."

And if things headed in the direction of her naughty thoughts, she'd be adding to Madame Eve's positive testimonials after all.

About the Author

Catherine Peace has been telling stories for as long as she could remember. She often blames two things for her forays into speculative fiction—Syfy (when it was SciFi) channel Sundays with her dad and *The Island of Dr. Moreau* by HG Wells. She graduated in 2008 from Northern Kentucky University with a degree in English and is still chasing the dream of being super rich and famous, mostly so she can sit around in her PJs all day and write stories. When not being a slave to the people in her head, she's a slave to two adorable dogs.

You can visit with Catherine at:
http://lexcade.blogspot.com

Also by Catherine Peace

Gemini: Disillusioned

Rocking the CEO

This Time Next Year